For Marissa —T. R.

randomhousekids.com

ISBN 978-0-7364-3345-7 (trade)
ISBN 978-0-7364-8220-2 (lib. bdg.)

Printed in the United States of America
10 9 8 7 6 5 4 3 2 1

Palace Pets

Teacup

Belle's Star Pup

By Tennant Redbank

Illustrated by Francesco Legramandi

Random House 🏠 New York

Teacup rolled. Teacup spun. Teacup pranced on two paws. Her show was almost done. Time for the big finish!

Teacup moved to the center of the terrace. She carefully balanced a cup on her head. It wobbled a little to the left. It wavered a little to the right. But it didn't fall.

Phew!

Teacup remembered a show when she hadn't done so well. The cup had fallen

and broken into pieces. That was the day Teacup met Belle. The princess had fixed the cup and given the puppy a home . . . here at the castle!

Teacup tossed her head. The cup flipped through the air. Once. Twice. She caught the handle in her mouth and set the cup on the ground. She could see the old cracks in it. It wasn't perfect anymore, but it was still her favorite.

"Bravo, Teacup!" Belle called.

All around her, Teacup's friends cheered. Petit the pony stamped her hooves. Princess Belle clapped. Chip, Mrs. Potts's little boy, yelled, "Hoorah!" Lumiere whooped. Mrs. Potts whistled.

Teacup wagged her tail. She loved putting on shows. She loved making others happy.

While Teacup bowed her head, Cogsworth hurried across the terrace. He stopped near Belle.

"Excuse me," he said. "A letter just came for you." He held out an envelope.

Puzzled, Belle opened it. As she read the note, her cheeks flushed.

"Oh!" she said. "Simone Dumont wants to come visit the prince and me!"

Teacup's ears pricked up. Simone Dumont?

"Dear, we don't know who that is," Mrs. Potts said.

Belle laughed. "Simone Dumont is an inventor!" she said. "My father told me all about her. She invented a machine to pick fruit from trees. But that's not the best part. Simone is my age!"

"An inventor!" Mrs. Potts repeated. "How clever!"

Belle's face grew serious. "Everything has to be perfect for her visit," she said. "I'm going to need your help, everyone."

The princess looked at Cogsworth. "Cogsworth, will you please get the castle into tip-top shape?" she asked.

Cogsworth bowed. "Certainly," he said.

Belle turned to Mrs. Potts. "Mrs. Potts, would you please cook up a feast?"

"Of course, dear," Mrs. Potts agreed.

Belle spun on her toes toward Lumiere. "Lumiere, could you please make sure Simone is comfortable?"

Lumiere kissed the back of Belle's hand. "With pleasure."

Then Belle crouched down until she was nose to nose with Teacup.

"Teacup, I have a special job for you," she said. "Will you perform for Simone? Your show? I don't want her to be bored while she's here. She's used to the

excitement of a big city! She'll love you!"

Teacup woofed and spun in a happy circle. Perform for an inventor? What an honor!

Belle kissed Teacup on the nose.

"Thank you all," she said. "I can't wait. Just think—Simone will be here in two days!"

"Watch out, Teacup!" Lumiere cried. He hurried by with flowers for Simone's room.

"Make way!" Cogsworth called. He directed several maids to the bedrooms.

"Has anyone seen the sugar?" Mrs. Potts asked. "My goodness, I remember ordering two sacks."

Teacup danced out of the path of a

broom. The grand hall was busier than the village square on market day! Teacup usually practiced her show there. But that wasn't going to happen today.

"*Pssst,* Teacup. Over here!" a voice called.

At first Teacup didn't see who had spoken. Then she noticed four white hoofs sticking out from the bottom of the drapes across the hall. The drapes moved, and a

white nose poked out. It was Petit!

To get to her friend, Teacup dodged a delivery boy carrying a crate of apples. She narrowly missed a kitchen maid dashing past with a bucket of ice. She ducked between the legs of a burly butcher. Finally, she was safe on the other side of the hall.

Teacup pushed aside the drapes with her nose. "Petit, what are you doing?"

"Trying not to get run over!" the pony said. "Last time I started across, the prince stepped on my tail." Petit snorted.

"Belle even put him to work! He's moving her dresses to the spare room."

Teacup laughed. She pictured the prince's face. He was kind, but definitely grumpy at times.

"Let's run for it," Teacup told Petit.

"Do you think we can make it?" Petit asked. She and Teacup watched a farm boy slip on a puddle of water. The chicken in his arms squawked and flew to the banister.

"We can't stay here," Teacup said. "It's dangerous!"

Teacup raced across the marble. She

leaped over the puddle of water. She skidded around a stack of buckets and scooted out the castle door.

Petit was seconds behind her. They collapsed together in a heap on the lawn.

"I've never seen the castle so crazy!" Teacup exclaimed.

"I'll be glad when it's normal again," Petit said. "After Simone's visit."

"Simone!" Teacup jumped to her paws. "I have to practice! Okay, Petit. I'll put on my show for you."

Teacup ran through the whole show, from the rolls to the balanced cup. When she was finished, she asked, "Well, what do you think?"

Petit nodded. "It was amazing, as always! And perfect! I don't know how you do it—all that rolling and tumbling." She stopped for a moment. "But—"

Teacup cocked her head. "But what?" she asked.

"But . . . is it *special* enough for Simone? It's the same show you did the other day. Maybe you can add something new?"

Teacup sat up on her back legs. Yes! Petit was right. She was so worried about being *perfect* that she hadn't thought about being *special*.

"Petit, you're so smart!" she said. "I'll add a new trick, one nobody has ever seen before!"

Teacup tried out lots of tricks.

She tried a front flip. But she couldn't quite make it all the way around.

Petit winced. "That looks like it hurt," she said.

Teacup rolled onto her back and held her paws in the air.

Petit wrinkled her nose. "Not exciting enough!" she said. "You're just lying there."

Teacup balanced a ball on her head. Then a spoon. Then one of Belle's shoes.

"Hmm . . . it's kind of like balancing the cup, isn't it?" Petit said.

Teacup stopped. The shoe thumped on the walkway. "It's hard to come up with a new trick!" she said.

She lay down in the grass. A bumblebee buzzed past her, headed for a flower. It reminded her of Cogsworth, bustling

around in the castle with so much to do.

The garden was as busy as the grand hall . . . just in a different way. Dragonflies hovered in the air, then darted off. By the back wall, a bunny nibbled clover in the sunshine. A frog leaped through the grass. When a stone blocked the way, the

frog leaped onto it and then over it.

"That's it!" Teacup said, sitting up. "Leaps! I'll add leaps to my show. The first thing I leap over will be small." She looked around. "Like that watering can."

The watering can sat next to the roses. Teacup took a running start and cleared it easily. Petit stomped her hoofs in support.

"The next one will be bigger." Teacup nodded at a stone bench. She ran. She leaped. She soared over the bench!

"The last one should be very big," Teacup said. "Hmm." She trotted through the garden. Finally, her eyes stopped on . . .

Petit!

Petit backed away. "Oh, no!" she said. "I'm too big. You can't leap over me."

"Hold still," Teacup said, moving toward her.

Petit shook her mane. "Nuh-uh. You could get hurt. *I* could get hurt."

But Teacup was already running. Teacup was leaping. Teacup was soaring. She was going to make it!

Or . . .

Maybe not.

The pup's paws snagged on Petit's back and she tumbled forward. But Teacup was a true pro. She landed and rolled and popped back to her feet. "Ta-da!" she said.

Petit swished her tail over her back. She would surely have a bruise there the next day.

"You know, Teacup," she said, "leaping is a great new trick. It's perfect. Really! But what if instead of leaping *over* something, you leaped *through* something?"

Teacup tilted her head to the side. "What do you mean?" she asked.

Petit nodded toward the top of the trellis. "Like a hoop," she suggested.

Teacup followed Petit's gaze up past the fountain . . . up past the garden wall. There, at the top of the wisteria trellis, hung a wooden hoop. In the spring, Belle laced colorful ribbons through it.

Teacup eyed the hoop. "What a great idea!" she said.

Teacup dashed to the fountain.

"Teacup, wait!" Petit said. "I didn't mean *that* hoop. Just one like it . . . but closer to the ground!"

Petit had a point. The hoop was high—really, really high. But Teacup needed a really, really exciting new trick.

"The hoop is perfect. Plus, I don't have time to look for another," Teacup said.

"Could you give me a boost, please?"

Petit sighed. She folded her front legs. Teacup leaped onto her back. Petit stood up.

Teacup jumped onto the marble fountain.

She balanced on the edge. Then she leaped onto the top of the wall.

"I wish I were a cat!" she called to Petit as she walked along the wall to the trellis. "They're good at climbing."

"Or a monkey," Petit said under her breath.

Teacup leaped onto the trellis. She carefully scrambled across the wooden slats. The hoop hung off the middle part. She scooted forward, but she could barely reach the hoop with her paw. She had stretched an inch more to poke at it, when—

SQUAWK!

A bird flew out of a nest in the wisteria! Its wings flapped in Teacup's face.

Teacup wobbled a little to the left.

She wavered a little to the right.

And then she lost her balance!

She toppled, nose over tail, down past the trellis and the wisteria.

She landed—*WHOOSH!*—in a soft mound of ivy.

KER-THOOP! The hoop clattered to the walkway next to her.

Petit rushed over.

Teacup shook ivy leaves from her fur.

"I'm okay!" she said. She stretched her paws to be sure.

"What a spectacular trick!" Petit said. "Maybe you can add it to the show."

"Or . . . maybe not," Teacup said. She couldn't imagine taking that fall over and over!

The hoop was worth it, though. While Petit held the hoop up, Teacup jumped through it forward. She jumped through it backward. She jumped back and forth through the hoop as Petit let it roll.

Teacup practiced all afternoon. She

practiced while the sun set. She practiced while the moon rose and the stars came out.

"Teacup," Petit said with a yawn, "isn't it time for bed?"

"You go," Teacup said. "Simone is coming tomorrow! I need to run through the show again. I was a second late on that last leap."

Petit shook her head. "You know, sometimes perfect is kind of boring," she said. She waved a hoof at Teacup and headed for the stables.

Teacup stopped. Was Petit right? Was she trying to be *too* perfect? Would anyone notice if she didn't jump through the exact center of the hoop, or if her leap was a little off?

Probably not.

But Teacup kept practicing anyway.

Teacup woke when the sun rose. She wasn't the only one up early. In the great hall, Cogsworth scrubbed a pesky dirt spot on the marble floor. In the parlor, Lumiere practiced charming smiles in front of a mirror. In the kitchen, Mrs. Potts was baking. She'd made enough treats to feed an army of inventors!

Teacup checked the library. Belle was pacing back and forth. An open book was on the table next to her.

Teacup jumped in front of Belle to get her attention.

"Oh!" Belle said, coming to a stop. "Good morning, Teacup! Are you excited about today, too?"

Teacup wagged her tail.

Belle kneeled next to her puppy. "I'm kind of nervous," she admitted. "I know it's silly. I just want everything to be perfect for Simone."

Teacup barked. She and Belle were a lot alike.

"Simone will be arriving in the village soon," Belle said. "Then she's coming here." She ruffled the fur behind Teacup's ears. "I can't wait to see your show. I know it will be wonderful!"

Teacup watched Belle leave the library. She was as excited as Belle. She wished Simone would arrive *now*.

Or . . .

Belle had said that Simone would be in the village soon. Teacup could go to town.

She wouldn't have to wait. She could see the inventor when she got there!

Teacup dashed down the hall, out the door, and into the woods. She was little, but she ran fast. She didn't want to miss Simone.

Panting hard, she skidded into the village square. She looked around. She saw the baker, the cheese maker, and the butcher. But where was Simone? Had she already come and gone?

Then Teacup heard the clatter of cart wheels on cobblestones. A wagon, driven by a girl, rolled into the village. In the back was a lump covered by a blanket.

"Bonjour!" the girl called. "Does anyone know the way to the castle?"

"Of course," said Marie, the baker's wife. "We know who you are, too."

Simone looked surprised. "You do?" she asked.

Marie shrugged. "Small towns have no secrets," she said. "Belle's father told us about you. And about your invention."

"I'd give anything to see it," the cheese maker added.

"Anything?" Simone laughed. "For some tasty cheese, I'll show you." She patted the blanket in the back of the wagon.

The cheese maker tossed her a wedge. "It's a deal!" he said.

Simone opened the back of the wagon. She rolled the invention down a ramp to the ground. She placed it under a pear tree at the edge of the square. Then she whipped off the blanket.

Teacup sat on her hind legs to see better. The invention was an odd-looking machine. Pipes, cranks, and levers stuck out in every direction.

Simone kneeled in the dirt. She pulled a wrench from her skirt pocket. "I just need to—" She tightened a bolt. "And a little bit here—" She pounded a nail with the end of the wrench. "Now . . . to start it up."

She turned to the villagers. They were

watching eagerly as she prepared.

"Are you ready?" Simone asked.

Everyone nodded.

Simone smiled. "Are you sure?"

More nodding. Someone yelled, "Yes!"

Teacup woofed. She knew what Simone was doing. Simone was putting on a show!

With a flourish, Simone hit a button. The invention rattled to life. A wooden arm unfolded. It closed around a tree branch and shook it. A pear fell off the tree and into a chute. When it slid to the end of the chute, it flipped into a pillowed

basket at the base of the invention.

"Oh!" the baker cried. "I could use one of those. My back aches from picking apples for tarts."

The machine picked more pears and flipped them into the basket.

Teacup had never seen anything so marvelous. And it gave her a great idea. She could make the invention part of her show!

She ran back to the castle, full speed all the way.

Teacup was back at the castle waiting with Belle when Simone's wagon pulled up. The inventor jumped down from the wagon. She made a curtsy to Belle.

"*Bonjour,* Your Highness," she said.

Belle rushed forward to hug her. "Your Highness? Please! Call me Belle," she said. She introduced Simone to the prince.

She introduced Lumiere, Cogsworth, Mrs. Potts and Chip, and Petit. She introduced Teacup.

Then Belle took Simone's hand and pulled her toward the castle. "I have so much to show you!" she said.

Teacup trotted at their heels. Belle showed Simone the library, the ballroom, and the tower. Then Simone set her invention up in the garden and turned it on for Belle.

Belle clapped. "It's wonderful! My father will love it!" she said. "But how did you get the arm to move like that?"

Simone grinned. "I'll show you!" she said.

Belle and Simone crawled under the invention to study the gears. When Belle came out, she had a grease smudge on her cheek.

Teacup barked happily. The girls in the village sometimes thought Belle was odd because she loved books so much. Simone was a perfect friend for Belle.

"Now, Simone, I have a surprise for you," Belle said. "A show!"

Belle winked at Teacup. That was her signal!

Simone sat with Belle on the garden bench. Cogsworth, Lumiere, Mrs. Potts, Chip, and Belle's father all gathered around. Petit grabbed a spot in the front row. The prince came to watch, too.

It was time to begin!

Taking a deep breath, Teacup launched into the show. She rolled. She spun. She pranced on two paws. She jumped through the hoop. She jumped through the hoop again as it rolled across the grass.

Next up—the super-special part!

With her paw, Teacup hit the button on Simone's invention. The wooden arm unfolded. It shook a peach from a tree and flicked it toward the basket.

But Teacup jumped in front of the basket and caught the peach in her mouth. She flipped it to her nose and balanced it there.

"Hoorah!" Simone yelled. She clapped loudly.

"Bravo!" Belle called.

Petit stomped her hooves.

Teacup felt a glow of joy. It was perfect!

Then something hit her in the ear. The peach atop her head wavered and wobbled. It fell to the ground.

What had happened?

Teacup turned—

In time to see another peach coming her way!

It smacked her right between the eyes.

Oh, no! She'd forgotten that the invention didn't pick just one piece of fruit. It picked one after another!

When the next peach started flying toward here, she ducked and it glanced off her back.

"Oof!" She heard a cry behind her. Teacup whirled around. Her eyes widened in shock.

The peach had hit the prince!

Teacup leaped onto the invention's start button. But instead of stopping, it picked peaches faster!

Peaches now zoomed across the garden. Lumiere jumped in front of an incoming peach and saved one of the maids from getting hit.

Cogsworth sputtered as a peach brushed the end of his mustache.

Petit hid behind the stone bench. She found Belle's father hiding there, too!

Simone raced over. She turned a dial on the side of the machine, and it clattered to a stop.

In the silence, Teacup's tail drooped. She had wanted everything to be perfect.

Instead it was all wrong! Would Belle and Simone be mad at her? Had she broken the invention?

Teacup wanted to hide. She didn't want to face her friends, but she had to finish the show. She always finished . . . even when things weren't going as planned.

Teacup returned to the center of the garden. She leaped as high as she could. She pranced like a dancer. Her rolls were faster than ever before. At the end, she balanced her cup on her head. Peach juice was in her eyes. But the cup didn't waver.

Instead of taking a bow, Teacup lowered her head and covered her nose with her paws. Then she heard a surprising sound. It was clapping. And whistling!

She looked up.

Why was Petit smiling? Why was everyone cheering?

The show was a mess. Her crown was crooked. Her fur was sticky.

And she had hit the prince with a peach!

Someone touched Teacup's paw. It was Simone. Next to her were Belle and the prince. Teacup couldn't face them.

"You, little pup, are amazing!" Simone said.

Teacup looked down.

Simone was being nice.

Simone raised Teacup's chin with her hand. "I mean it," she said. "You're just like me. You have spunk. Things didn't go your way, but you kept going."

Teacup lifted her head higher.

Maybe perfect *was* boring at times. And imperfect things could be special, too. She glanced at the cracked cup by her feet.

"All your shows are wonderful," Belle said. "But, Teacup, this was the best! When that peach hit the prince . . ." Belle's shoulders shook with laughter. "It was priceless!"

"Hey," the prince said. "It wasn't *that* funny!" He picked up Teacup and playfully tossed her in the air. When he caught her, Teacup licked his face. He tasted peachy.

Teacup wagged her tail. It was her worst show ever. But maybe it was also the best.

She had no control over whether it

rained or not. She couldn't control an invention if it went crazy. Sometimes things didn't go the way she planned. But she could control one important thing: what she did next. She could keep going. She could do her best.

Sun or rain, perfect or not, Teacup could always shine!